PLANET OMAR

EPIC HERO FLOP

PLANET OMAR

EPIC HERO FLOP

ZANIB MIAN

ILLUSTRATED BY
KYAN CHENG

putnam

G. P. PUTNAM'S SONS

G. P. PUTNAM'S SONS
An imprint of Penguin Random House LLC, New York

First published in the United States of America by G. P. Putnam's Sons,
an imprint of Penguin Random House LLC, 2022
Text copyright © 2021 by Zanib Mian
Illustrations copyright © 2021 by Kyan Cheng
First published in Great Britain by Hodder and Stoughton, 2021
First American edition, 2022

Visit us online at penguinrandomhouse.com

Library of Congress Cataloging-in-Publication Data
Names: Mian, Zanib, author. | Cheng, Kyan, illustrator.
Title: Epic hero flop / Zanib Mian ; illustrated by Kyan Cheng.
Description: First American edition. | New York : G. P. Putnam's Sons, 2022. |
Series: Planet Omar ; book 4 | Summary: "When Omar takes the blame for a few
small things to keep his friends out of trouble, he feels great—until something
big happens and everyone thinks Omar did it"—Provided by publisher.
Identifiers: LCCN 2021059835 (print) | LCCN 2021059836 (ebook) |
ISBN 9780593407172 (hardback) | ISBN 9780593407189 (epub)
Subjects: CYAC: Humorous stories. | Muslims—Fiction. | Schools—Fiction. |
Friendship—Fiction. | LCGFT: Humorous fiction.
Classification: LCC PZ7.1.M514 Ep 2022 (print) | LCC PZ7.1.M514 (ebook) | DDC [Fic]—dc23
LC record available at https://lccn.loc.gov/2021059835
LC ebook record available at https://lccn.loc.gov/2021059836

Printed in the United States of America
ISBN 9780593407172
1st Printing

LSCC

Design by Tony Sahara
Text set in Averia Serif Libre

For all the children who remain their best selves

through life's ups and downs.

CHARLIE

DANIEL

Still trying to
stay out of trouble

Can always
make us laugh

Mr. McLEARY

Principal
Also known as Mr. McScary
Can be super unpredictable
Reads boring books
z z z

ELLIE

Perhaps a funny grandma in disguise?

SARAH

I can never tell what she is thinking

JAYDEN

Has great taste in pencils

ADAM

Can hold his breath for a really long time

CHAPTER 1

The sound broke through

the pin-drop silence of the classroom.

It was the sound that was the start of the

WORST TWO WEEKS OF MY LIFE.

We were having a computer lesson, and my

best friend Daniel couldn't wait to show me the

new crazy video he had been talking about, of

a lion being friends with a human and saving

her from an attack by a hyena. I had said he could just email me the link and I would watch it at home, because I knew that our computer teacher, Mr. Philpot, would go absolutely bananas if he saw us.

But Daniel said, "No way. I can't live through the WHOLE day without showing you. It's only one minute long anyway."

And he hit the PLAY button with the sort of look on his face that my little brother, Esa, has when he's farted and he's waiting for everyone to smell it.

But it was the WORST idea possible, because:

- we are not allowed to watch videos in class.

- we forgot to plug in our headphones, so EVERYONE heard it.

- THE VOLUME WAS ON ((«FULL BLAST»)).

Ellie even screamed and jumped out of her seat before she figured out it was just a video. I guess she thought a real lion had somehow come through the door.

Our other best friend, Charlie, was staring

at us from across the room, where he was

working with his partner, Adam.

HIS EYES TRIPLED IN SIZE.

Mr. Philpot was scanning the few

computers around us to make up his mind

who to shout at.

You haven't met Mr. Philpot before, so I will tell you about him. Remember Mrs. Crankshaw, the substitute teacher we once had instead of our lovely usual teacher, Mrs. Hutchinson? The really mean one? Well . . . Mr. Philpot made her look like a  baby lamb wrapped in cotton candy with a drizzle of extra-nice sprinkles on top.

When Mr. Philpot shouted, you could hear him from the other side of the school building. And even if he wasn't shouting at you, you would still shiver in your boots.

The good thing was that it only happened

every so often, not all the time. I guess some things really made him blow his top, and other things didn't so much. We hadn't figured out what they were yet, but Charlie was on it. Because Charlie likes math so much, he sees patterns and common factors in everything, and he said, "There must be a common factor in all the times Mr. Philpot has exploded. We just have to figure out what it is so we

NEVER, EVER, like, EVERRRRRR do it.

But with the video, I thought we might have done it. I looked at Daniel and saw the horror in his eyes as Mr. Philpot took big fat steps toward us. Daniel used to be a mega-bullying

TROUBLEMAKER, but those days are behind him. He hasn't been in trouble for a long, long time, and I know how happy that makes him. But now he would end up back in the principal's office like he used to be ALL the time before we were friends.

I saw a tear trickle down his cheek as he put his hands on his ears to prepare for Mr.

Philpot's storm, and I knew I had to do something . . .

CHAPTER 2

I looked at Mr.
Philpot, who
was wearing his
usual shorts with
sandals. He had
knobby knees, and
something about
them made me imagine him as an
covered in poisonous warts. This ogre
was about to eat my friend.

8

I stood up really fast. My legs felt all 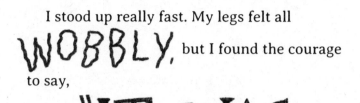 but I found the courage to say,

My hand went up to make super sure Mr. Philpot knew who to blame.

"You??" he said. He said it like he didn't believe it.

"Yes, me, sir. I did it; you can shout at me in my face, if you want."

That made somebody at the back giggle, but they quickly stopped when Mr. Philpot turned his poisonous warts toward them.

The whole class was looking at me.

That means around sixty eyeballs in total.

I could see Daniel from the corner of my eye. His hands had moved from his ears to his mouth, covering his shock at what I was doing.

Mr. Philpot didn't shout. Instead, he said, "Can I see you outside, please?"

So I followed him as he walked toward the door. I turned around to look at Daniel, who looked relieved, scared and super confused all at the same time.

When we were outside the classroom, Mr. Philpot said, "Now, young man, what has gotten into you? What a ridiculous fuss you've caused! This isn't like you at all."

"I know, sir. I'm sorry. It was sort of an accident, I guess. I was trying to

catch my , which had taken off into the air as if by magic, and . . ."
I babbled on, trying to imagine ways a video could be played by accident.

"OK. OK. Well, don't do it again, please, Omar. You're a good kid."

And that's it! I was let off the hook. No principal's office, no earth-shattering shouting, no anything at all.

With a wide smile of relief, I walked back to my seat next to Daniel, who could still be Daniel-the-kid-who-used-to-be-a-troublemaker-but-is-now-a-totally-awesome-well-behaved-kid instead of Daniel-the-naughty-kid-who-has-gone-back-to-his-bad-ways. That made me feel

really super fantastic.

I had helped my friend and everything had turned out great.

When it was time for recess, the first thing Charlie said to me was,

"Omar, YOU are a hero!"

Daniel said, "I can't believe you took the blame for me! It was so crazy! I always knew you were cool, but I never thought I would ever have a friend that cared so much he would get in TROUBLE for me."

OK, now

I felt awkward and shy because Daniel and Charlie were making it a big superhero deal. So I did a handstand to distract them. I had been practicing at home and had only broken one lamp in my mission to get really good (and the telling-off I had gotten from Dad was totally worth it).

It worked. Charlie and Daniel started clapping and trying to do their own

handstands,

which they weren't quite managing just yet.

Soon other kids from our class were coming up to me to ask what happened. And when they found out it wasn't really me who had played the lion video, but that I'd taken the blame so Daniel wouldn't get into trouble, they all looked at me as if I had burped a rainbow or something.

For the rest of

the day, I got

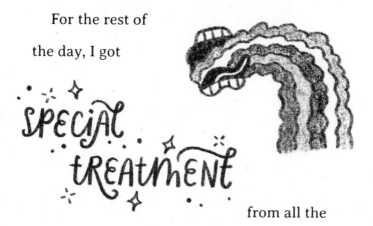

SPECIAL

TREATMENT

from all the

kids in the class. The best things were:

- Sarah let me cut in front of her in the lunch line.

- Jayden gave me his Pokémon pencil.

- And Adam even asked if I wanted to play soccer with him, which he has never done in the history of my feet stepping into this school.

CHAPTER 3

Back at home, I didn't mention what had happened at school to Maryam, my annoying big sister, but because she knows me so well, she noticed something was different.

"What's up with you? Why are you taller or happier or something weird like that?"

"I'm not," I said. My secret was grinning through my eyes, even though my lips were straight.

"You probably answered some geeky science question right at school and now

you're showing off!" she said, walking away to show she didn't care anyway.

Maryam hates that I like science like my mom and dad, who are scientists, because she's not interested in it and always messes up on

SCIENCE SUNDAYS

(which is when our whole family does fun experiments at home in the kitchen).

I was putting all my school stuff away in the bedroom I share with my little brother when I heard wailing from down the hall. Esa was clearly not in a good mood. He was doing that thing where he cries and talks at the same time, so it comes out all squeaky and high-pitched.

I went to see what he was mad about this time, and it was because Mom had flushed the toilet when he was finished, but HE had wanted to flush it.

"BRING BACK MY P💩💩S!"

he was crying. "I wanted to flush them! Bring them back!"

Mom looked a bit tired. Maybe she needed

one of her energy balls. She makes them out of dates and nuts, which is boring. So when I eat them, I imagine that they have more fun ingredients, like the milk of a winged horse and a drop of honey made by bees that live underwater in a lake called

the Pool of Powerful Energy.

That makes me feel extra strong when I've eaten one. Imagination makes everything more exciting.

"Do you need an energy ball?" I asked Mom,

who looked like she was trying very hard to calm Esa down by explaining that once the poos are gone, they are gone.

"Yes, please!" she said.

So I went to get her one, and as I put the hard brown ball on a plate, I tried NOT to think about how it sort of looked like poo. Imagining food as poo is something I would get seriously told off for if Mom knew. So I thanked Allah she couldn't hear my thoughts, put the plate on Mom's favorite tray (it's pink and flowery) and took it upstairs.

Mom was so pleased with me, she gave me a great big hug. "Sometimes you do the exact right thing at the exact right moment, Omar. Thank you!"

I love Mom's hugs, even though I never let

At home, so no hijab

her hug me in front of my friends.

I did something nice for someone again, but it made ME feel just as good as it made Mom feel. That's funny, right?

I went back to my room to go and play with the R🔩B⚙T I had coded with Dad, when I saw something out of place—a deck of cards that was signed by an astronaut Dad met years ago at a science conference. (He thought I'd like a present signed by an astronaut, and the only thing he had in his pocket was a pack of cards. Don't ask why. Dad always has

strange things in his pockets,

things you'd never ever guess.)

And now the cards were sitting by my robot. So weird!

I was sure this was Maryam getting me back for running down the stairs screaming the other day, pretending there was a mouse in her room just for fun. So I went straight to her room and asked, "Hey, Maryam, did you move my cards?"

"No! Did you even see me go to your stinky room?!" she said.

"No . . ." I said.

And she was right. I hadn't seen her anywhere near my room since we had gotten back from school.

SUPER WEIRD.

CHAPTER 4

The next day, as I walked to school, I wondered if Mr. Philpot had told Mrs. Hutchinson about the lion video. I know that teachers gossip a lot behind the doors of the mysterious staff room, but I had learned my lesson about eavesdropping on them from the time

Staff room

I misheard some gossip and thought that my teacher had been taken by

ALIENS.

Anyway, I was really hoping he hadn't said anything, because I really like Mrs. Hutchinson, and I wouldn't want her to think I did anything **naughty**.

As I walked in, she smiled her usual smile at me and winked her usual wink, which made me think, **PHEW,** she doesn't know. But the most important clue of all was that her hair waved its usual hello. It wasn't her disappointed hair. I know exactly what her disappointed hair looks like, because I saw it last week when Ellie forgot to feed the class goldfish when it was her turn.

Charlie had his worried eyebrows on. They were scrunching down and close together. I tapped them to make them go back to normal eyebrows, but they wouldn't.

"What is it, Charlie? Who did it?" asked Daniel. Daniel still sometimes thinks that the reason for all problems happening is someone else being mean.

"Nobody did it . . . It's my grandma.

She's really sick," said sad Charlie.

"Is she going to die?" asked Daniel.

I whacked him on the arm.

"What?" he said.

"You can't say things like that..." I said.

But it was too late, because Charlie

was already sobbing, and hot tears were

trickling down his face.

Mrs. Hutchinson was at his side in a flash.

She took him outside to have a chat, and we all

sat down to read our books, wondering what

she was saying to him.

When Charlie came

back, his worried

eyebrows were gone, but his toothy

grin still wasn't anywhere to be seen. Daniel and I made our minds up to bring it back by lunchtime.

Our task for the morning was to learn about mindfulness and what we do to be mindful. And the reason was that a fancy team from a fancy TV studio were coming to make a news report about it, and they were going to interview kids and teachers at our school.

"I've never been on TV before!" whispered Daniel, super excited. "But I don't know what  is."

Mrs. Hutchinson was asking the class what we thought it was. "Hands up if you can tell me."

Daniel shot his hand up even though he had just told me a second ago he had no clue.

"It's when you make your mind full! Like, just think of as many things at the same time that you can; think about your sick grandma and your homework and why Ellie said your breath smelled last Tuesday and how nice Mrs. Hutchinson's hair is. Everything! Mind full." He finally stopped, extra proud of himself.

I wasn't sure what mindfulness was, but I was sure it wasn't *that*.

Ellie and Sarah burst out laughing and started whispering to each other and laughing even more.

Daniel had turned jelly-bean red. And I could tell something terrible was going to erupt from his trembling lips, so I quickly said,

"THat's exactly wHat I tHinK, too."

It was a lie, of course, but I thought it was a good lie, because I could see he felt better right away.

"Exactly! It's what it sounds like," Daniel added.

Mrs. Hutchinson said, "Don't be so rude,

girls." Then she said to Daniel, "Thank you for trying to make sense of the word, Daniel. I'm always very impressed that you're never afraid to try."

Now Daniel **blushed** flamingo pink and completely forgot about Ellie and Sarah.

Mrs. Hutchinson explained that mindfulness was actually the activity of noticing what is happening in the moment you are in now, to help you focus or feel better about something. It could be counting your breaths or watching how the wind rustles the leaves in the trees.

I wondered if she had done something to do with mindfulness with Charlie when she had talked to him outside.

For our task we had to think about what we already do to be mindful and plan what we would say if the camera crew chose to interview us. Mrs. Hutchinson said she was sending permission letters home for our parents, but that the TV crew would only choose a few of us to talk to, and it would help if we looked

NEAT AND TIDY.

I tried to make my brain work super hard, but I couldn't think of anything I do that's mindful, because I don't normally use the things in the real world to calm down; I use my imagination instead. (You might remember that sometimes I conjure up my amazing dragon, H_2O, when there's a really bad situation going on . . .)

Daniel spent most of the morning worrying about whether he looked neat and tidy enough or not.

"Don't worry," I said. "We've still got a few days till they come."

As we walked out into the playground at lunchtime, there was a loud ambulance siren screaming in the streets. That was normal and happened all the time, but today it sent Charlie into a complete and utter breath-stopping panic.

CHAPTER 5

"What if it's for my gran?!" Charlie said each word like it was stuck in his mouth. His hands were shaking.

P😟OR CHARLIE.

Daniel and I both put our arms around him as we walked over to the school pond. It was Daniel's turn to test the pH levels of the water, and it would be my turn next week.

"It's not for her," said Daniel.

"How do you *know*?" said Charlie.

"Charlie, think like you do for math. What

are the chances it's for her?" I said.

But that didn't help, because Charlie started crying. "The chances are

BIG —
they're HUGE —
because she's <u>so</u> sick."

I felt so sad for Charlie that my own heart started hurting. It felt like there were tiny little trolls in my chest using it as a punching bag. And if I felt that, Charlie's heart must have felt like a thousand T. rexes were using it as a trampoline.

Other kids were starting to stare.

"Come on," I said, "let's go back to the classroom."

We could help Charlie calm down in there, and maybe Mrs. Hutchinson could do some mindfulness with him.

"OK," said Charlie.

He walked with us like he was some sort of

not really there.

"So much for making his toothy grin come back," Daniel whispered to me.

"It will come," I said. I really hoped so because I didn't want my friend to be sad forever.

• • •

Ellie and Sarah were eating in the classroom, and Adam was showing them how long he could hold his breath. Mrs. Hutchinson wasn't there.

"You're not supposed to eat in here," said Daniel.

"So? What are you going to do? Are you going to *tell*?" said Ellie.

"If you do, we'll tell Mr. Philpot who *really* played the lion video," said Sarah.

Ouch. Sarah is really scary sometimes

Angelic on the outside and mean on the inside.

"What's wrong with Charlie, anyway?" asked Ellie. "Has he lost one of his freckles?"

"None of your business," said Daniel, who wasn't happy about being threatened.

Charlie was at the window. Probably wondering if the

ambulance had gone to his grandma's house.

Nothing I was saying was making him feel better. So I just stood next to him while Daniel tried to make the girls leave.

They were loving the chance to tease Daniel by not leaving, and he was falling into their trap.

"Charlie! They're not leaving. Aren't you angry? Don't you want them to go?"

I knew Charlie did want them to go, but he never gets angry. Charlie has a few moods, but I've never seen him actually angry the way Daniel and I can get.

"All right, I'm going to try it for longer this time!" Adam was saying, but nobody was really paying attention.

The girls were walking

extra s l o w l y

to the door, with their drinks in their hands.

"Oh no, I can't walk faster than this—I'm stuck in something," Ellie said, balancing on one foot and laughing her head off.

But that wasn't as smart as she thought, because within seconds, her bright red fruit punch was all over the floor.

"SEEEEEEE!" said Daniel as we all gathered around the puddle to stare.

"Get a mop!" Ellie screeched.

But it was too late, because just then our principal, Mr. McLeary, walked into the room.

The six of us were frozen in our spots, all staring at the principal. He was staring at the red puddle. Nobody made a sound, except Adam, who suddenly took in a big gasp of air.

Would we all get in trouble? Or just Ellie? Would we have to say it was Ellie? Would she say it was her?

I looked at Ellie. She had never looked so scared before. I remembered how good it had felt when I had taken the blame for Daniel the day before, so, without wasting another second, I stepped forward.

"Sorry, sir. It was me. I know we aren't allowed to eat in here, so I'm very sorry, and, erm . . . I won't do it again."

I heard Mom's voice in my head: *Sorry means you won't do it again.* (But does it? Because I have been really, super-duper sorry about things but then done them again and been sorry again and tried not to do them again but forgot.)

"Well, this is **DISAPPOINTING,**

Omar, and so unlike you," Mr. McLeary was

saying through my daydream. "Why did you

think you could have a drink in your classroom?"

"He brought me upstairs to see Mrs.

Hutchinson because I was upset about my sick

grandma," piped up Charlie.

"Yes, because her chances are very big!" said

Daniel, which got confused looks from everyone.

"Oh . . . I see. Oh, well, I'm very sorry. Hmm. It seems like you were taking good care of your friend, Omar. But stick to the rules next time, and get this cleaned up," he said as he walked off, checking his watch.

"WOW! Omar, you got away with it again!" said Daniel.

"Thank you, Omar," Ellie breathed, throwing her hands together and bouncing up and down. "Thank you, thank you, thank you! You are *literally* a hero!"

"Like Spider-Man!" said Sarah.

"We need to get him a T-shirt that says 'Super Omar'!" Charlie said, and FINALLY his

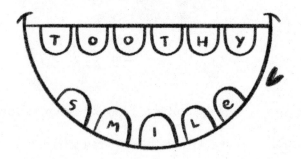

came back.

"Ah, it's nothing." I sheepishly scratched the back of my head. But secretly I did feel super cool.

A very purple-looking Adam, who everyone had forgotten about, said, "I held it for a minute this time . . . Oh, never mind." And then he walked out.

Mrs. Hutchinson came back to the classroom after that, rubbing her tummy (she's having a baby soon, so she does that a lot) and looking tired. Right away she told me that Mr. McLeary had told her what had happened.

"It's a shame that the principal had to speak to me about one of my best students." She sighed. Her hair was lifeless. "And then there was yesterday, too."

HUH?
SHE <u>DOES</u> KNOW ABOUT THAT?

I hung my head and tried to imagine her hair singing and dancing.

She stood there for a second. I knew she felt

sorry for me, so I looked up at her and tried to smile. She patted my head and said, "It's OK. Chin up."

But my chin was very heavy now, and all I wanted to do was stare at my shoes.

CHAPTER 6

I was going to use the weekend to think more about  so I would know what I was talking about next week if the TV crew spoke to me.

I was waiting for a nice, calm moment to ask Mom and Dad about it. Calm moments are super rare in our family.

On Saturday, we went on our usual trip to the *Mosque* to pray, then we went shopping for groceries and **HALAL MEAT.** حلال

You can get halal meat in the supermarket usually, too, but there aren't always very many choices, so sometimes we go to the halal butcher instead.

Dad waited outside in the car because the

smell of the meat counter makes him gag, and while Mom was distracted, talking to the butcher, Esa took a bite of every peach in the fruit and vegetable display.

"For the love of bananas in pajamas! What have you done?!" said Mom when she noticed.

"No nice ones," said Esa. "I wanted a nice one!" And he pointed at the peaches as if they had been naughty.

Maryam and I burst into giggles.

The man behind the counter was not laughing. He was very angry. "Don't you feed your child at home?" he asked.

The silly question made the whole situation funnier to me and Maryam, and we only stopped laughing when Mom gave us a

deadly glare.

"Of course I feed him. It's not because he's *hungry*," said Mom. "I'll pay for all of these, don't worry."

"I am worried," said the funny man.

Mom handed him some cash and didn't even wait for the change. She gets **embarrassed** about things a hundred times more than other people. Knowing Mom, she will never go back to the same shop again.

Dad found the whole thing hilarious. He laughed all the way home, which eventually made Mom laugh, too.

We told Mrs. Rogers, our next-door neighbor, when she popped over for tea, and she laughed till her eyes watered, and gave Esa a great big hug.

Maryam whispered to me that it wasn't fair that Esa got hugs and giggles when he was naughty. She thought he got away with too much. Usually, I would have said something like,

"Right?! It's not fair!"

But I kept my mouth shut, because the last couple of days I had gotten away with things, too. They were things *I* didn't *actually* do, but the teachers didn't know that.

We decided to play a game of Monopoly after we **gobbled up all the pakoras** that Mom had made us for a snack. They're fried, and that's probably why they do extra-yummy things inside my mouth.

I passed Mom on the stairs on my way up to get the Monopoly, and I slipped a bit, but luckily Mom caught me.

"Thanks, Mom." I grinned.

"You're welcome. I'm just your friendly neighborhood Batman."

"Spider-Man." I groaned. "It's

"Same thing!" she said. Even though she knew it definitely was not the same thing.

I shook my head at her the rest of the way to my room and thought about how everyone at school was calling me a *hero* but also how disappointed Mrs. Hutchinson was. It wasn't easy being your friendly neighborhood anything.

I opened my closet to get the Monopoly and was super weirded out because the astronaut playing cards were now sitting on a pair of my folded jeans.

WHHAAᴬAAAᴬAT?

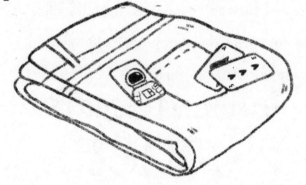

Who keeps moving these cards? And why?

I went straight to Maryam, the cards in my

hand, and said, "Maryam, stop it. You did it again. You moved these!"

"What's going on?" said Mrs. Rogers, who was hanging out in her favorite armchair, watching over Esa while Mom and Dad were upstairs for the evening prayer.

"Maryam keeps moving these cards around my room and pretending it wasn't her," I complained.

"I told you it wasn't me. You can ask Mrs. Rogers; I haven't even been upstairs since we got back from shopping," said Maryam, complete with *innocent sparkly eyes* and everything.

"She was right here," said Mrs. Rogers, nodding.

"Well, how are they moving to different spots

in my room, then?" I asked them.

"Beats me," said Mrs. Rogers. "Maybe they are moving all by themselves." And she gave me one of her confusing smiles.

The last thing I did before the end of the day was call Charlie to check how he was. I was $Super$ relieved

to find out that the ambulance hadn't been for his gran, and that she was starting to feel better again. I could hear Charlie's toothy grin in his voice through the phone.

"You won't believe this, but the ambulance WAS for my street, though. Apparently some kid got his head stuck in the TOILET!"

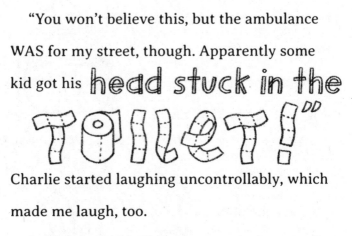

Charlie started laughing uncontrollably, which made me laugh, too.

I think I was laughing even more because I was happy my friend was happy again.

CHAPTER 7

Sunday came around super fast, and I

realized that I had forgotten to ask my

parents about

because of how busy Saturday had been.

As you'll probably remember, on Sundays we

have SCIENCE SUNDAYS

in our house. I was really looking forward to

this one, because we were going to be making

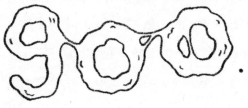.

Goo is actually useless, if you think about it.

But it's pretty useful to have hours

of fun **Sludging** your fingers

(and feet when Dad lets me) in a

STRANGE SLIMY SUBSTANCE.

As I waited for Mom and Dad to finish what

they were doing, I imagined all the things in a

fantasy world that might be gooey:

- Definitely a dragon's booger (except H_2O, because he's special and so clean that his boogers are just soapy bubbles).

- Troll babies. I imagined that they are actually born as goo and slide around across the floor until they're about one year old, when they start growing ugly troll features.

- Unicorn tears. Yep, I made unicorns yucky in my imagination, and that's because I'm sick of seeing them on everything.
Once, I went to a shop and I could have sworn my eyeballs became unicorn-shaped just from seeing them on all the things they were selling.

"Right!" announced Dad, holding up the dye we were going to use for the goo. "Ten points for guessing if this is booger green or mushy-pea green, but be warned, whichever one you guess, you have to eat it for dinner tonight."

"Don't encourage that kind of silliness," Mom said, trying to hide her smile.

"Ah, you know you love it." Dad winked.

"Booger color!" said Esa.

"Ewwwww, you have to eat boogers now," pointed out Maryam.

"No! You!" said Esa, and he didn't think twice about throwing a spoonful of yogurt at her.

"DAAAAAAAAD! Look what he's done! I bet you're not even going to tell him off."

"Esa, food is not for throwing," said Dad.

"Say sorry to Maryam."

"But I want to do it again," said Esa. "Sorry means never do it again, remember, Daddy?"

Dad couldn't help but chuckle.

"We can't laugh at all the naughty things he does, darling," said Mom, swooping Esa off to talk to him in the other room.

I just wanted the fun to begin, but as usual, there were too many

SHENANIGANS

happening. Well, at least I hadn't guessed mushy-pea green . . . If I had to have them for dinner, I would not be a happy Omar!

When we finally did the experiment, it was so much fun. Mom and Dad, being the

BRILLIANT SCIENTISTS

they are, had figured out the chemical that toy makers put in that powder you get to put in the bathtub. If you've ever seen it, you'll know that it's so much fun!

The water in the tub grows and grows as it becomes this slimy goo. It's because of a type of chemical called

a polymer

(that's "pol-eeeeee" and "mer"). This polymer basically loves water, so it sucks it up. Some

polymers

hate water, so they don't

suck it up at all, like the stuff plastic

cups are made of. That's why they're made of it,

obviously.

I couldn't help imagining different types of

polymers as little fluffy monsters who either

hate mushy peas, so don't touch them, or

love mushy peas, so gobble them all up. You

know which kind of monster I am. Charlie is

the complete opposite:
a gobbling one. I don't
know how he does it.

Later that Sunday we
prayed together in the house.

Mom and Dad pray
five times a day—
at dawn,
midday,
afternoon, sunset
and night—

but us kids don't join in every single time, and
sometimes we just do it ourselves in our own
rooms. It's the same routine at home as at the
mosque, but instead of there being hundreds
of people, there's just Mom, Dad, me, Maryam
and Esa. Dad does the prayer by saying bits

of the **Qur'an** out loud, and we all do the motions: hands on knees, hands and nose on the floor, then back up again with hands folded in front of us.

Esa always messes it up, because he has no concentration span. Actually, he does, but it lasts twelve seconds. After those twelve seconds, he either jumps on Dad's back when it's the nose-on-the-floor stage, or stands under me when it's the hands-on-knees stage,

with his silly smile inches away from my face,

or, worst of all,

he farts out loud.

The problem with all this is that we aren't

allowed to laugh during the prayer, and do

you know how hard it is not to laugh when

you know you're not allowed to laugh and

something funny happens?

It is HARD, and I don't always

manage. And if I burst into giggles during my

prayer, Mom and Dad get very angry, so I get

in trouble for something Esa started.

Maryam struggles, too, so we talked about

what to do.

I suggested we lock Esa in the other room when we pray, but Maryam said that would be animal cruelty and then laughed a lot at her own joke. I said it wouldn't be cruel if he was happy in there, which he would be if we threw in some chocolates and toys.

Anyway, as you can see, Sunday was full of busyness, too, so I completely forgot to ask about mindfulness. I only remembered when I walked through the school gates on Monday morning.

YİKES!

What if the camera crew chose me and I had no clue what to say?

CHAPTER 8

"Mrs. Hutchinson, when are the TV people coming?" I asked as soon as I saw her.

She smiled. "Well, good morning to you, too."

"Oh, sorry, good morning." I was embarrassed. I had forgotten my manners, which is something I never do with Mrs. Hutchinson, because she brings out all my *Pleases* and *thank-yous* and *excuse-mes.* She even brings them out in Daniel.

She patted my head and said, "They're coming tomorrow."

PHEW. I was safe for now.
I gave Mrs. H my best smile
and decided to impress her with super-
good behavior because of her thinking I did
two naughty things last week.

We poured into the classroom, and I realized
someone was missing.

"Where's Daniel?"

I asked Charlie.

"Don't know. Late, maybe? Or sick?"

Awww man, I hate it when one of us is sick
and not in school. There always seems to be
something we can't do because we're not a
complete group.

But just then, Daniel walked in, his whole

face red as a beetroot. I don't mean red like

when he gets angry, I mean,

WHHAAᴬAᴬAᴬAT?

DiD YOU RUB BEET JUiCE On YOUr FACE?

kind of red.

The whole class gasped and whispered and looked at Daniel as if he had grown a mermaid's tail.

He slid into his seat next to me and opposite Charlie and said, "Why do these things always happen to me? Huh? Can you tell me, guys?"

"Erm . . . *what* things *happened* to you, exactly?" said Charlie carefully, almost as if the red face would pop if he chose the wrong words.

I tried to imagine what would come out if it did pop. Red M&M's? Or something more like

gruesome red zombie blood? Maybe Daniel had been bitten by a zombie, so zombies were the things that had happened to him?

"I tried to look **neat and tidy** for the cameras," said Daniel. He used his fingers to make air quotes so that Mrs. Hutchinson's words "neat and tidy" sounded like a mythical creature. Something people could never be.

"You tried to look neat and tidy by painting your face red . . . ?" I said, not stepping as carefully as Charlie.

"No! I used a stupid face wash. My mom's! And it made my stupid face red!"

"Oh, come on . . . Your face isn't stupid," said Charlie kindly.

"Are you suuuure?" said Daniel. "Not even *now*?" He pointed at his funny-looking face.

Charlie and I tried to exchange a look without Daniel seeing. Neither of us wanted to pop the zombie blood.

I tried to think of something helpful to say.

"Maryam had an **ALLERGIC REACTION** once, when she ate too much candy every day for fourteen days. But Mom gave her an allergy pill and it got better pretty much, very almost right away."

(Actually, it still took at least twenty-four hours to get better, but Daniel didn't need to know that.)

"Oh?"

My fib had worked. This "oh" was hopeful.

"What's this magic pill? Can I have one?"

"Sure, I'll ask Mom," I said. And then I got lost on my own planet for a bit. I couldn't help but imagine myself as George from Roald Dahl's book, mixing up a marvelous medicine for Daniel. I had always imagined the crazy things I would put in mine, but I never actually did it because my brother is truly silly enough that he'd take a sip when I wasn't looking, and I'm afraid it might do something a lot worse than make him grow.

After wisely giving Daniel some time to get over the fact that he had walked into a classroom in front of thirty kids with a red face, Mrs. Hutchinson came over to our table to talk to him. Of course she wanted to know what on earth had happened to him and if he was OK.

"I'll be fine after I've had my magic pill," said Daniel. Which was funny and worrying at the same time, but I quickly explained to Mrs. H what he meant.

We didn't focus much on our work that morning. Daniel continued to tell us how angry he was when he saw his face in the mirror. I tried to cheer him up by telling him and Charlie all about my SCIENCE SUNDAYS and how cool it is when the powder turns everything into a big growing gloopey mush.

"Wow, that sounds so cool," said Daniel.

"I'm going to do it at home, too," said Charlie.

"Do it! All you need is the

It's really super easy. I could bring some in for you."

The other kids in the class were only half focused on their work, too, and very distracted by staring at Daniel and listening to what we were chatting about. Daniel's red face seemed to be the most interesting thing that had happened since Mr. Philpot's shouting had shattered the fish tank. (We weren't totally sure whether it was the shouting that did it, or whether some kid had knocked it over at exactly the same time. I guess we'll never know.)

Mrs. Hutchinson let us get away with being too distracted to work because of Daniel's sensitive situation, but she kept telling the others to stop being nosy and get on with their tasks.

The nosiness didn't stop all day. It drove Daniel absolutely nuts. We were followed around the playground at lunchtime like the royal family are followed by PAPARAZZI (that's a fancy word for people who want to take photos of famous people—usually to catch them doing something that would make great gossip).

Ellie and Sarah kept walking by on purpose and giggling loudly.

Adam came up and tried to ask us to play soccer again, but Daniel thought he just wanted to be close enough to see his red face, so he told him to go away.

"I'M SO ANNNGGGRYYY

Daniel said, stomping his feet. "It's not fair."

Then, suddenly, becoming aware of his own

stomping, he looked at Charlie's feet, which he had never seen stomping before. "What makes you angry, Charlie?" he wondered out loud.

"I don't know," said Charlie.

"Racism?" I tried. "Plastic in the sea?"

"Yeah, of course. That makes everyone angry," said Charlie.

"But that's not in just one moment. What makes you feet-stomping, eyeball-popping, table-smashing, car-crashing *angry*?" said Daniel.

I LAUGHED. "Nothing, because he's not the Incredible Hulk."

Charlie laughed, too. "Yeah, nothing ever makes me *that* angry."

Daniel turned around to see at least fifteen kids in their little crowds watching and pointing at him.

"Well, I'm bursting. I think I might turn green and big instead of red."

He was sort of right, because by the time we got in from lunchtime, Daniel was so angry, he put his fist into a nice ripe banana sitting on Mrs. Hutchinson's desk. You can imagine what THAT looked like.

Mrs. H came in, again looking like she hadn't really rested during her lunchtime. Or maybe the baby in her tummy was making her tired. The banana was probably part of her lunch. She looked super disappointed.

"Who did this?" she asked.

The class was silent. Daniel was squirming in his seat but not saying anything.

I had vowed to be good, but my best friend was already suffering a lot.

One last time won't hurt too much, I told myself.

And with a great lump in my throat, I put my hand up.

CHAPTER 9

The teachers all thought I had turned into a

TROUBLEMAKER.

I could imagine them having conversations in the staff room.

Imaginary teacher 1: What's gotten into that Omar kid lately?

Imaginary teacher 2: He's behaving very unusually.

Imaginary teacher 3: Trouble magnet, if you ask me.

But with the kids I was a hero, and they

kept telling me so during after-school
basketball club.

When I shot a basket
with no net, Jayden said, "Cool
guy! Cool hero guy!"

"Omar never actually misses," said Ellie
proudly, as if she was my grandma or
something.

Adam hovered around me, even when I
didn't need to pass him the ball. "Is it cool
being a hero?" he asked.

"Erm, I . . . don't know," I said awkwardly.

"I would take the blame for someone, too,
you know. If I had the chance," he said.

"I know." I smiled at him.

And then Daniel and Charlie randomly

started chanting, "Who's a hero? O-O-Omaaaaaar. Who's a hero? Omaaaar!"

Daniel was so thankful, he kept using his mom's phone that evening to send me messages on my mom's phone.

Daniel

> Omar, thanks for doing the thing you did for me 😌 👀

He was trying to be secret in case either of our moms read over the messages later.

Me

> It's cool.

Daniel

> Oh, by the way, Mom knows what those magic pills are but she can't give me one cuz I have a bad reaction to them. 😭

Me

What? Only you would have an allergic reaction to an anti-allergy pill! 😄

Daniel

I know, right? It's not fair!

Me

See you at school tomorrow. Be sure to be "neat and tidy." Hehehe. 😄

Daniel

I'm not coming. There's no way I'm getting caught on camera with a red face.

Me

Awww man! OK . . . Get well soon!

Daniel

Thanks. Gotta go.

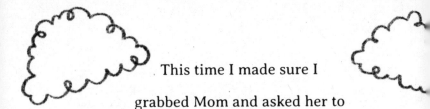

This time I made sure I grabbed Mom and asked her to tell me what we do at home for mindfulness.

She thought for a bit and said, "You know when I tell you to look at the clouds, and for a few minutes we just get lost looking at how fluffy

the clouds are and how the wind is moving them and how magnificent *Allah* must be if simple clouds are so glorious?

That's

mindfulness.

For those moments, everything melts away and we are only thinking about what's happening at that time to the thing we are looking at. Using our eyes to be aware of that moment. We can also use our other senses to be even more mindful, or we could notice our breathing by counting as breaths move in and out of our lungs."

"So basically it's forgetting everything else to really notice what you're doing right now?"

I said, trying to understand.

"Right! Perfect!" said Mom.

"Is it only when you stare at clouds and things?"

"No, no. It can be while doing anything if you get good at it."

"Oh, so wait a minute . . ." I said. "Are we supposed to do it when we're praying? Because Dad tells us to concentrate on the prayer and stop thinking about other stuff."

"Yes, exactly." Mom smiled. "So if you could manage to only think about you and Allah being there and melt everything else away, you wouldn't laugh at Esa's silly antics when you're praying!"

"Maybe I still would because what Esa's doing while we pray is in the *now*."

"Oh yes, good point, SMARTY-PANTS but if you really focus, you can tune out things in the now that you don't want to focus on."

"How??"

"Just focus on your breathing and the words being recited."

"Wow, cool. I'll practice when we pray tonight."

So later, when Dad came home at the very minute when it was time for evening prayer and didn't even have time to take off his leather motorcycle trousers before we prayed,

I tried to focus on how the air was going in and out of my lungs so I wouldn't think of anything else. Like why my astronaut cards were now sitting on my windowsill (they had moved again, and Maryam had denied doing it again), or how I was supposed to look neater and tidier than normal for school tomorrow (though I think I'm pretty neat every day, since Mom won't let me wear even my most favorite jeans if they have a tiny stain on them).

But, anyway, I was trying *not* to think of those things and only to listen to the words Dad was saying out loud from the Qur'an. I also had to not let my ears focus on the **Squeaky** noises Dad's pants were making every time he had to kneel down. Luckily, Esa was busy scribbling in his *How to Train Your Dragon* coloring book.

Mindfulness is really hard! But I think I managed to focus more than I normally do when we pray. *Maybe I'll get better if I practice every day*, I thought as I went to grab a bag of chips to take to my room.

Technically I'm not allowed to eat in my room, but if there was a chance they might pick me to speak to for the TV show, I really needed to poke around in my closet for my best *Minecraft* T-shirt while I ate them.

AHA! When I stepped into my room, I caught

Maryam with her hand in my drawer!

And that's when we had a

BIG FAT
INCREDIBLY
GINORMOUS
FIGHT.

CHAPTER 10

Maryam has to be the most annoying big sister EVER. I knew that she was just pretending that she wasn't the one moving the cards around, and then she wouldn't even admit it when she was caught.

"I'm just looking for 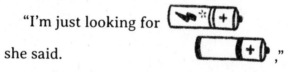 ," she said.

"You don't even let me *breathe* near *your* room!" I said.

Dad came in to ask what all the fuss was about. I didn't bother telling him because

Mysterious Maryam would deny it to him, too, and I couldn't be bothered.

But I stayed annoyed at her all evening and all night in my sleep, and I was *still* annoyed when I woke up and ate my breakfast.

I stayed annoyed until I realized that if I was going to be prepared for my day at school with the TV crew around, I had to find a way to not let her bother me and figure out what was going on with the cards later. I was also worried about how Mrs. Hutchinson would be feeling about me after the banana incident, which wasn't helping me to feel prepared, either. I almost decided that I needed to imagine my dragon, H_2O, on the walk to school, but then I realized I should just try to do the

magic instead! I looked up at the clouds to take my mind off my worries and only think about what was going on *right now*.

I was so busy looking at the clouds that I almost bumped into Charlie at the school gate. He was walking like a rigid robot and had the strangest look on his face.

"Charlie?" I said.

"They're here." Charlie tried to speak without moving his lips and pointed at the camera crew in the playground with his eyes.

"What?" I laughed. "We are allowed to walk and talk and be normal, aren't we?"

"Yes, but I'm really scared they will talk to me. So I'm trying not to attract attention to myself," said Charlie.

"I'm scared, too," I said, only just realizing how true that was.

"It's all right for you—you're a hero; you're brave," said Charlie.

I giggled. "I'm not actually very brave. I think I just made myself be for a minute even though I was super scared!"

Luckily, Mrs. Hutchinson wasn't acting differently toward me. When we talked about the banana, I had explained it was an accident: there was a killer spider in the classroom and I had tried everything to squish it, but it went and crawled onto her desk, and I had squashed her banana while trying to put my fist down on the spider. I don't like lying and don't do it very much, and I worried that my huge imagination made my lies

too WACKY,

but it seemed like maybe she had believed me.

I thought back to our conversation.

"So you go for killer spiders with your bare hands . . . ?" Mrs. H had asked, one eyebrow reaching for the ceiling.

"Erm . . . yeah. To save my friends."

"And where is the spider now?"

"Dead. Super dead."

"Well, thank goodness for that."

What do you think? Did she buy it?

This morning, Mrs. Hutchinson's hair was not hiding the fact that she was really excited about our school being part of this important news report on TV. Her curls were extra bouncy and were acting as if they were dancing to a happy song.

She didn't make us do normal work. Instead,

she gave us a little drama lesson so we wouldn't be nervous about the TV crew. They'd be filming all day, all around the school, and although the teachers had chosen some kids to interview beforehand, the TV crew might also talk to any kid wearing a red sticker, which showed they had permission to be on TV.

Charlie was wearing a red sticker, but as we walked out into the playground for lunch, he tore it off and looked at me with a face like the emoji who is very proud of what it's just done.

I half wanted to tear mine off, but I was one of the kids the teachers had chosen for them to interview, and I couldn't let Mrs. H down after all my attempts to be a hero.

I tried to act natural and went to visit the school pond to do my job.

I wish Daniel was here; he usually does this for me, I thought as I turned my nose away from the smelly pond while I checked the water.

I could have sworn one of the frogs stuck its tongue out at me, but maybe it was just eating a fly.

After that, Charlie and I walked around the playground with extra casualness until the TV crew came up to me with a big fluffy microphone and cameras the size of goats.

My legs were shaking. I didn't quite understand how they were still managing to hold me up as I stood there and talked about what mindfulness is to me. I tried to say about the clouds and the praying, but I don't know what I actually said. I don't even know if I spoke English.

I was glad it was over. I spent the afternoon

lessons feeling like my normal self again, instead of my worry-filled self.

But it didn't last long, because Mr. McLeary burst into the classroom and said,

"THE SCHOOL POND HAS TURNED INTO A HUMONGOUS PINK SLUSHY GOO!!!"

And thirty kids, a teacher, and the principal

all turned to stare at ME!

CHAPTER 11

My heart was bouncing and beating so fast, it felt like it was trying to escape out of my ribs.

All the faces stared at me with their minds made up.

OMAR DID iT.

Omar *was talking nonstop about goo powder science, and* Omar *was on pond duty.*

Before I knew it, I found myself in a place I had only heard stories about from Daniel: on the naughty chair in Mr. McLeary's office. I was squirming and wriggling while the principal acted as if there was a really bad smell in his office as he tapped my mom's phone number into a thing called a

Landline.

It's called that because it's a phone stuck to a piece of land. In this case, the land of Mr. McScary's Office for Wrongdoers.

But I wasn't a wrongdoer, and I felt really, awfully sad

listening to Mr. McLeary telling my mom about a terrible thing that I DIDN'T DO, as if there was proof that I did it.

I couldn't hear what Mom was saying, but she was obviously surprised.

"Well, he's been acting up lately, and all the signs point to him without a shadow of a doubt," said Mr. McLeary.

He was going to make even Mom believe I had done it.

All my heroics to try to help my friends were epically flopping in my face.

I was trying to think of what to do and what to say.

I couldn't tell the teachers that I HADN'T played the video, I HADN'T spilled the fruit punch and I HADN'T squashed the banana. Because then everyone would think of me as a snitch instead of a hero. If I HADN'T done those things, I'd have to tell the teachers who actually did them, and I wasn't going to do that.

Mr. McLeary said that Mom and Dad were going to have to come into school to have a chat with him as soon as they could.

After that, I did the walk of shame back into the classroom and was surprised and really happy to see a clear-faced Daniel. I

plopped

myself down at my table with my two best friends, who seemed like the only two people who didn't think I had put goo powder into the pond.

"You came in!" I said. "Your face looks better."

"Yep, it feels fine now. Charlie told me everything . . . This smells fishy, doesn't it?" said Daniel.

"Do you think someone is trying to frame you?" asked Charlie.

"Maybe. But it's not just me—all those poor pond creatures have lost their home! Who would do such a horrible thing?" I said.

"Horrid Henry?" suggested Daniel.

"Yeah, but the fact that

he's a pretend character kind of makes it hard for it to have been him." I smiled even though my heart was so sad.

"You're not the only person in the world who knows how to use goo powder," said Charlie.  "Why are they acting as if it was definitely you?"

"Well, Mr. McLeary said that it was pretty obvious it was me, and he even asked Mom what we did on SCIENCE SUNDAYS, and Mom had to say we used goo powder."

"Yikes. It does really sound like it was you," said Daniel. "*Was* it you?" he joked.

"HEY!" I protested.

I kept looking over at Mrs. Hutchinson, and she wouldn't even look at me.

Daniel put his arm across my shoulders and said, "We're going to have to find who did it and stamp on their toes!"

"Or prove that I didn't do it."

"You need an alibi," said Charlie.

He was right: an alibi is what I needed. But it would be super tricky, because I *had* been at the pond around the time it happened.

I looked down at the table, trying to think hard, and that's when I noticed Daniel's white sleeves had pink stains on them!

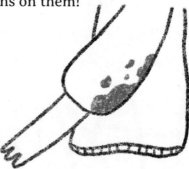

CHAPTER 12

I felt like I couldn't breathe.

All the way home, Mom was asking me

what had happened, and did I do it, and why

did I do all those other naughty things, and

what's gotten into me lately, and was it the same reason

I'd been fighting with Maryam, too?

But I couldn't pay attention. All I could

think about was whether it could have been

Daniel.

Maybe he couldn't help being naughty;

maybe it was still
inside him like a
big growly monster
trying to escape. Or
maybe he was jealous
because everyone was
calling me a

heRO.

He HAD come in
late. He could have
easily done it without
being noticed.

"NO!" I shook my thoughts out of my
head angrily. My best friend would
never do that to me in a million years.

"Excuse me, young man! How dare you say

'no' to me. You're already in a lot of trouble," Mom said.

"No, not you. Me. I was saying it to myself. Sorry," I told her.

"Well, that sounds silly," she said.

"I know, but it's true."

I hung my head. Everyone was mad at me.

That evening we had a family meeting. Even Mrs. Rogers joined in because she had come over to help Mom bake cookies for people at work.

Dad was TOTALLY serious.

He's only serious about 4.5 times each year.

The last time he was this serious was when somebody had robbed Mrs. Rogers's house while she was having dinner with us. He went straight out and got security cameras to install at her place and ours.

"Tell us everything in your own words," said Dad as we all sat around the dinner table.

I looked at Maryam's face. She seemed to be enjoying this a bit too much, probably because we hadn't made up since our fight.

I took a big gulp and started talking. I knew it was going to sound unbelievable . . . FOUR things had happened. I didn't do the first three, but I had said I had, and I didn't do the fourth one and I never said I had.

Mom and Dad listened carefully while I talked.

Mrs. Rogers got up for some water while I

was babbling on, and a small but **Squeaky**
fart escaped her as she
stood up.

I carried on with my story
but watched my family's
faces turn from serious to
embarrassed, losing focus on me as they
pretended not to notice.

"What's wrong with you all? It's just a fart;
everyone does them!" said Mrs. Rogers.

"I can't seem to hold mine in at this old age."

Everyone let their relieved giggles loose
and tried to focus on me again. But she had
released some of the tension, and Dad's face
wasn't as serious as it had started off.

I looked at Mrs. Rogers. She winked at me.

WOW!

She had actually farted on *purpose.* I loved her for that.

"So . . . do you believe me?" I finished.

Maryam spoke first. I was scared of what she'd say, but she said, "Fruit punch. You never drink fruit punch; you say it tastes like unicorn pee, so I believe you."

(You might be wondering how I know what unicorn pee tastes like. I used my imagination.)

(And no, not everything I imagine is that gross.)

"She's right. I believe you, too, Omar. Taking the blame so your friends don't get in trouble is just like you," Mom said, almost proudly.

"You shouldn't have done it, though. You should have helped them out some other way . . ." said Dad, not quite wanting to let me off so easily. "You wouldn't be in this mess if you hadn't lied all those times. Lies always come back to bite you; do you see that now?"

I did see . . . because now I was in a big, complicated, messy mess.

CHAPTER 13

Walking into the principal's office with your parents is the scariest thing possible.

Scarier than finding a spider on your towel when you bring it to your face.

Scarier than farting in public (which Mrs. Rogers will tell you isn't so scary after all).

Scarier even than speaking to TV cameras.

And I was doing it that Wednesday morning.

Mom and Dad were sure they were going

to convince Mr. McLeary that their son was innocent. They believed I was innocent, and they thought that two adults talking calmly to another adult would work magic.

But Mr. McLeary is one of those people who makes up their mind and nothing can change it.

"I understand that you're sure Omar didn't do this, because he's usually a good boy. A fantastic child, actually. But kids change. I'm sorry, but I've been doing this job for fifteen years, and I have seen perfect angels turn into fungus-filled tomatoes . . . so unless you can show me some proof, Omar is going to have all his lunchtimes in my office for a week."

"Whatever happened to innocent until proven guilty?" said Dad.

"This isn't a courtroom," said Mr. McScary.

And no matter what Mom and Dad said, he wouldn't change his mind.

WHHHOOOA.

A week of eating my lunches with McScary??!! I had to find proof I didn't do it, but I didn't know how I was going to do that.

I couldn't walk back to my classroom fast enough to talk to my friends and figure out an action plan. But on the way, I couldn't help but think of Daniel's pink sleeves again.

As I walked through the door, Daniel was asking, "What makes you angry, Charlie?"

It seemed like he was obsessed with this question. I guessed that maybe it's because Daniel isn't always the best at controlling his temper.

"I don't know . . ."

Charlie was trying to concentrate on the math he was supposed to be doing.

"I have to spend lunchtimes with Mr. McScary for a week," I announced with a lump in my throat as I sat down. I wasn't going to cry. Not in front of the whole class.

"But that's so unfair!" said Charlie.

"What? How can they make you do that?

I'M SO ANGRY,"

said Daniel. Then, with a flicker of hope, he added, "Are you angry, Charlie?"

"Yes," said Charlie. His eyebrows looked like they were trying to be angry but didn't know how. He banged his fist on the table a few seconds too late for it to be believable, which made me giggle.

"We don't have to be angry, guys; we have to be smart and figure out a way to prove it wasn't me."

I peeked at Daniel to see if he looked guilty at all, and I hated myself even more for being suspicious of my friend.

CHAPTER 14

We decided we were going to try to talk to
other kids to see if they might have seen or
heard something, or even know who actually
turned the pond into pink, slushy, gooey slime.

Golden Time gave us the perfect opportunity—
it's the moment in the week when we are allowed
to move around the class, sit where we want
and do what we want, reading, drawing, making
something . . . It's usually
loads of FUN, but today
we were on a MISSION.

"Did you see Omar at lunchtime yesterday,
like, not next to the pond?" Charlie asked Jayden,
hoping someone would give me an alibi and say
that I was somewhere away from the scene of the
crime the whole time.

"I saw him in the playground, but I also saw
him coming back from the path to the pond,"
said Jayden.

He was right. I was at the pond. I even touched

the pond, but I didn't put goo powder in it.

"Do you want me to lie, though? I could lie," he said with an over-the-top wink.

"NO!" I said quickly. "No more lies."

Lies are like glue particles. The more you have, the stickier things get. I was already stuck enough.

Eight kids in the class said they saw me coming back from the pond. Five of those eight offered to lie since I had been a hero for other people.

Filip said he saw me in the school library for the whole hour of lunch. *What??? Hahaha.*

Adam said, "Maybe it won't be too bad with

McScary?" Which was stupid because it was obviously going to be the worst thing ever.

Ellie and Sarah said they actually saw me pour the goo powder into the pond very clearly with their own two eyes. And then they said that even heroes get into trouble in the best movies.

"Yes, and then one of the lying bad guys gets eaten by the monster!" said Daniel.

"I can't believe they would lie like that!" I said, walking back to our table and resting my head on it.

"What would Sherlock Holmes do if finding an alibi didn't work?" said Charlie.

"Find out who bought goo powder in the last few days?" I said.

"Impossible!" said Daniel. *Was he scared we would find out HE had bought some?*

"SOGGY CORNFLAKES!"

shouted Charlie excitedly.

"Erm, random . . . ?" Daniel said.

"That's what makes me angry!"

"Soggy cornflakes?! Really?" I said.

"Yes, it makes me so angry when they go soggy WHILE I am eating them!" Charlie said, and sure enough he was turning red just with the thought of it.

"Oh, I like it," said Daniel, grinning like the Joker. "Bad soggy cornflakes. So yucky and mushy!"

"Yeah!" said Charlie, feeling proud that Daniel was so amused.

"Who would have thought? Out of all the things that make people angry, yours is soggy cornflakes." Daniel was laughing so hard that the sip of water he was drinking went up his nose instead of down his food pipe.

"Ouch, ouch, it hurts." He was scream-laughing.

I laughed so much the sides of my own body started hurting.

Daniel was just the best. I was being so stupid thinking for even a minute that he might have done it. I felt like such a bad friend. It was more likely that I would wake up with four legs than that my best friend was the reason I was in so much trouble. So I just blurted it out through my giggles:

"You know, Daniel, I sort of thought you slushified the pond because you had pink stains on your sleeves yesterday."

Daniel stopped laughing faster than a calculator does math. His face looked as white as a ghost all of a sudden, which was a funny difference from the color it had been the other day.

"But I know it's not you!" I said quickly. I wished I had never said anything at all.

"It was calamine lotion, OK? I wanted to put calamine lotion on my face, and I couldn't open the bottle, so it went on my sleeves," Daniel said sadly, and he got up. "I thought we were friends, Omar. I should have known it was too good to be actually true."

He walked away just as the bell rang. I was left feeling like a super-soggy cornflake as I made my way to Mr. McLeary's office for my first lunchtime behavior-fixing session.

CHAPTER 15

"It was awful!"

I found myself pouring my heart out to Mrs. Rogers at her kitchen table after school while she fed me all sorts of sugary goodies to comfort me.

Mom says you shouldn't use food to make yourself feel better, but it seemed to be doing an all right job. So I took another mouthful of a triple-chocolate brownie and sprayed crumbs onto Mrs. Rogers's cardigan as I complained about the mess I was in. "And so,

just like that, I was the biggest pond-wrecking,

heartbreaking supervillain in school."

Mrs. Rogers seemed to find that funny.

"You're no SUPERVILLAIN, Omar, that's surer than the nose on my face. But you need to tell Daniel how sorry you are and how much you love being his friend."

"I tried! But he wouldn't even talk to me after lunch. He was giving me the silent treatment, pretending he couldn't see me, even when I did his favorite impression of a snake with legs."

"Things always have a way of working themselves out, Omar. You've seen that happen many times. Like the time  you and Daniel were lost on the London Underground. That was terrible while it was happening, but it made you the best of friends in the end," said Mrs. Rogers the Wise.

She was right. I felt a lot better and more hopeful as I strolled the few steps back to my house. This was like the bigger-picture thing that Dad is always going on about. He says that even if something feels hard and horrible at the time, *Allah does it for a reason* because it all fits together to make something happen that is great for us in the end. Like a jigsaw puzzle that comes together to make a really nice picture. Even the bits of the puzzle that look ugly on their own are needed to make it whole.

I felt so good thinking about life as a jigsaw puzzle that I picked a flower from our front yard to give to Maryam.

"Thanks for helping me with the fruit punch thing yesterday," I said, feeling cheesier than ever as I launched the flower at her, imagining it for just a second as a rocket.

"Wow, you must really be suffering if you're acting this soppy," said Maryam.

To my surprise she scooped me up in a big-sister hug, and, even more to my surprise, I started sobbing into her arm.

Mom and Dad saw and were **VEry worried about me.**

It was super weird seeing them act like boring, normal people instead of messing around and giggling and saying cheesy things to tease their kids. All they could talk about was how unfair it was, and how they couldn't just let it go, and how maybe they should talk to the

school board.

I don't really understand what the school board does, but the way my parents were talking about them, they seemed like mysterious creatures who control what's happening in a school. I imagined them all sitting around a table in a meeting room. They had long, flowy white hair or big white beards down to the floor and curly black hats that had round pencils at their tips and wrote down all the rules.

"Omar shall be set free," one of them was writing.

That night, although I had been feeling a bit better, when I was alone in my bed in the dark, the worries of what was happening came back. I tried to use my *mindfulness*

to only think of what was happening to me right then. But my other thoughts were too loud, and my brain was flashing all the questions at me.

CHAPTER 16

As I waited to see Daniel in class the next day, I had a lump in my throat the size of the mountain in Wales my parents made us climb last summer.

I'm usually someone who comes up with great plans, but for this I had nothing. I didn't know what I would say to him. I was hoping just saying "Be my friend" would work, but maybe I would have to do something like in the movies and pay someone

to fly a hot-air balloon over the playground with "Be my friend, Daniel Green!" on its side.

I mentioned both of these ideas to Charlie, who said, "Erm . . . one's too much, and one is not enough. Maybe try something in the middle?"

Whatever I was going to do, I had to do it before I was sent to McScary's office at lunchtime. But then Daniel walked in with a huge smile on his face.

WHHAAᴬAAAAᴬAT?

"He sat down next to me and said,
"Be my friend."

I was in complete hysterics at the joy of Daniel making things better and at the funny way he happened to say just what I was going to say to him. It's as if he was in my head. That's what makes us such good friends: we do and say a lot of stuff the same way.

"**PHEW**," said Charlie. "I couldn't sleep last night worrying about you two not being friends!"

"But I don't get it. I thought you'd be mad forever!" I said to Daniel.

"Well, I was definitely planning to be! But I told my little sister, Suzy, all about what happened, and she basically told me off like she was a little grandma!"

"Hahaha, why?"

"She hit me over the head with a stuffed unicorn and said, 'You're such good friends! And he's only in this accidental trouble because of *you* and that video you played and the banana you squashed. And think of all the awesome things you've done with him and Charlie!' And

THEN she completely flipped and held my best

sneakers over the toilet and said,

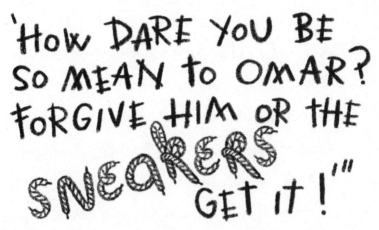

'How DARE YOU BE
So MEAN to OMAR?
FORGIVE HIM OR THE
SNEAKERS
GET IT !'"

said Daniel, doing his best Suzy impression.

"Soggy sneakers!" Charlie giggled.

I laughed. "She's brilliant!"

"Yeah, I'm sorry, Omar," said Daniel.

"Noooo, I'm sorry. I was being such

a brainless hamster," I said.

And we did a sideways

sitting-down hug.

Mrs. Hutchinson was telling the class that the news report was going to be on TV on Sunday.

"I still don't understand what *mindfulness* is," whispered Daniel.

So Charlie and I explained everything we had learned about it. I talked about trying to focus on your breath and said that you could count it going in and out of your lungs.

"Ohhhhhhhhhhhhhh, right," said Daniel. "Nope, I *still* don't understand!" Which had our table in loud, uncontrollable laughing fits once again.

Mrs. H walked up to our table. "Boys, are you ready to study history or stand-up comedy over here?" she joked.

But she didn't give me her usual wink and special smile, which reminded me that

HA HA HI HA HA HA

although things were good with Daniel again, my favorite teacher still thought I had turned into a TROUBLEMAKER.

I finished my worksheet on medicine in the olden days in complete silence. I wished there was a pill I could give the whole world to make them see the truth. A truth-seeing pill, so no kid would ever have to go through what was happening to me. But then I wouldn't ever be able to tell kind lies, like when Maryam asks if she looks nice in her red strawberry lip gloss and I say yes.

Before I knew it, it was lunchtime. I watched everyone run out of the door to the playground while I carried my lunch to the principal's office.

"Don't worry, Omar. We're going to spend lunchtime figuring this out for you," Daniel and Charlie said before they left.

Mr. McLeary opened the door and stood aside to let me walk past without a word.

Have you ever sat in a room with someone when neither of you is talking? It's super awkward. So I said, "Nice shoes, sir." Even though they were the second-ugliest pair of shoes I had ever seen.

"Oh, are they? Would they look nice filled with pink goo?" replied Mr. McScary, looking unimpressed.

OK . . . I thought. *I guess I'll have to sit in silence.*

I wasn't allowed to do anything except read. But I forgot my book, so I had to borrow one from Mr. McLeary, who was eating a sandwich I had seen a fly sit on seconds earlier. Somehow I didn't feel so bad about not telling him. He would tell me off if I did, anyway.

I had read somewhere that flies lay their eggs on food, and their eggs are basically maggots. So when he choked a little on his food and coughed, my imagination made me see maggots falling out of his mouth. It was super disgusting and made me not want to look at him anymore.

The book was called *The History of Politics*, and it was actually more boring than sitting and staring into space.

OH YEAH! All this chaos made me forget to find out how the astronaut cards were moving . . . I was sure it was Maryam; I just had to work out how she had made them move when she had Mrs. Rogers as her alibi. I would be a detective when I got home. I had a plan.

I spent the rest of the hour imagining what life would be like in space, which actually made

the time fly by.

After lunch, Charlie and Daniel spent the class winking at each other and putting their fingers to their mouths in a "shhh" action.

"What's going on, guys?" I asked.

"Absolutely nothing," they said.

"It doesn't seeeem like nothing," I said, curious. Nothing seems like nothing when someone says it's absolutely nothing. But they just wouldn't say what it was.

All they said was,

"Don't worry, Omar.

After today, you're never going to have to worry again . . ."

CHAPTER 17

When I got home, I grabbed an apple and went to my room to put my plan into action—to find out once and for all how my astronaut cards were moving around.

Maryam had promised it wasn't her . . .

And Dad had promised that ghosts didn't exist . . .

My dragon, H_2O, was imaginary and only did things I made him do . . .

I put the cards on my desk and crawled

under my bed and got ready to lie low (literally) for a while . . . Well, I didn't tell you that it was a fantastic plan! But at least it looked like there was nobody in my room.

And I'd be able to see who came in to move the cards.

I took a bite of the apple.

CRUUUNCH!

Oops, too noisy. I was going to have to stay very quiet for this to work. It was super boring, but I stuck with it.

Finally I heard footsteps walking in very slowly . . . I pricked up my ears and opened my eyes wide, like a rabbit hiding from a fox.

I'd recognize the feet . . . I waited for them to appear . . . *Wait, what?* They were Mom's feet walking in. Was it *her*? But no, it was a false alarm. She had just come in to hang a shirt in my closet.

I waited some more.

Suddenly, there was a very fast movement. Someone whizzed into my room so fast I didn't see the feet, and they raced around, jumping from place to place, making it super hard for my under-the-bed head to follow. It was ESA! And he ran out as fast as he had run in! He was like that little kid from *The Incredibles*. But why was he in such a hurry?

It was his room, too. Surely HE wasn't moving the cards? That seemed way more planned than a three-year-old could manage. How did he get so tricky?

I quickly crawled out from under the bed to check, and, sure enough, the cards were now on my bookshelf.

That little . . .

But Mom's yelling broke through my thoughts.

"OOOOMMMMMAAAAARRRRRR! Come downstairs this minute!"

YIKES!

What was it? Mom only calls like that if I'm in

EPIC TROUBLE

What had I done now?

"I just had a call from Mr. McLeary.
Apparently, after school today, Jayden from your
class went to him to say that you were with him
the whole time during lunch on Tuesday, so you
couldn't have wrecked the pond. But when Mr.
McLeary explained what would happen to him if
he was lying, he crumbled and confessed on the
spot that he WAS lying!"

WHHAAᴬAAAᴬAT?

"Did you put him up to it, Omar? Because

that's what Mr. McLeary thinks."

"Of course I didn't! I said no more lies!"

And then it all made sense. That's why
Charlie and Daniel had been so funny and said
that I wouldn't have to worry again. They'd put
Jayden up to it!

"Well, now Mr. McLeary is really angry,"
said Mom.

She kept talking, but I could only hear her
in the background through the
fog of my own scary thoughts.
My best friends had only been
trying to help me, but this had
made things a gazillion times
worse than before. And things
were TERRIBLE before!

"Oh, Allah, help me!" I
whispered.

When I heard Dad's motorcycle rumble outside just in time for dinner, I ran to the door. This was one of those moments when only one of his big, strong hugs would do, and I wanted to catch him when he was still in his leather motorcycle gear. Somehow, the smell of it made me feel like everything would be OK.

"This looks really bad," Dad said when Mom filled him in. "If they were even slightly unsure

before about Omar being guilty, they will be dead sure now."

"Yeah, only a guilty person sends a friend to lie for them," said Maryam.

Everyone was as gloomy as me. They felt helpless about not being able to get me out of this.

"I'll go and talk to the principal again tomorrow," said Dad, poking at his food and not eating it, exactly the same as me.

"I'll go with you. I think my son, John, went to school with Mr. McLeary back in the day. Maybe some old memories will soften him up," said Mrs. Rogers.

I was desperate to see them all normal again. It would help me feel better, too, so I took a sip of my fizzy lemonade and said, "Hey, Dad, did you know that if you have a fizzy drink, then burp and sneeze at the same time, it feels like there's a firework up your nose?" And I fake-smiled.

Dad fake-smiled back. I could tell because his eyes didn't go wrinkly, and I felt so sad at all this trouble that I thought I might throw up.

CHAPTER 18

That night, as I was wondering if Mr. McLeary would increase my punishment and how Mrs. Hutchinson's hair would have flopped sadly over her shoulders when she heard about Jayden, Dad came into my room and sat on my bed.

"You know who's in control of everything, don't you?" he asked.

"Mr. McLeary?"

"No." Dad chuckled. *"Allah.* He's in control of Mr. McLeary and all of us and everything that happens. I just wanted to remind you to trust in Allah's plan, and ask Him for help, because He can show you the truth."

"OK," I said.

"Remember the jigsaw puzzle?"

"Yes, Dad. I have one of the ugly pieces right now."

Dad laughed again. Yes! That was twice, and his eyes had wrinkled, too. I felt a bit better. He helped me pray to Allah before I slept, and tucked me in just like when I was little.

"I'll make a caterpillar in a cocoon out of

you!" he joked, wrapping me in my duvet.

. . .

The next morning, as we left for school, Mom said, "Smile, Omar— trusting in Allah means you don't need to worry about it anymore."

So I smiled at her as best as I could.

Dad and Mrs. Rogers couldn't speak to Mr. McLeary because he had gone to some principals' conference in Oxford. But he had left instructions for what should happen to me for the extra lying and mischief he thought I had been up to.

Omar will have lunch in my office for a second week. In my absence he will have lunch with Mr. Philpot, and he may no longer sit next to anybody in the classroom until further notice.

YIKES!

First I have to sit alone, and *then* I have to sit with Mr. Philpot? Having lunch with Mr. Philpot was worse than being stuck with McScary for an hour. What if I did something to make him blow his top?

Charlie and Daniel ran up to me in the playground as I was waving goodbye to Dad and Mrs. Rogers. They felt super bad.

"I feel worse than Thor would feel if he had to wear a tutu," said Daniel.

"Worse than a lactose-intolerant person covered in cream cheese," said Charlie.

"Worse than someone who scratched a million-dollar Lamborghini," said Daniel.

"Worse than—"

"OK, guys, stop!" I said. "You were trying to be helpful. I get it, and I'm not mad."

"Phew, thank you!" they said together.

"And don't worry about Mr. Philpot," said Charlie. "I think I've figured out the formula. He always blows his top when these things happen together:

1. He is hungry. He's only ever blown his top before lunchtime.

2. Whatever naughty thing a kid did, when they weren't immediately sorry for it."

And he scribbled on a piece of paper for me:

HUNGER + NAUGHTY KID WHO'S NOT SORRY

= TOP BLOWN

"Well, he'll be having his lunch when I'm with him, so I think I'm OK . . ."
I said, hoping it was true.

"Yeah, just don't even breathe before he puts it in his mouth," said Daniel.

I sat at a desk over in the corner all morning, feeling sorry for myself. Mrs. Hutchinson didn't look at me once. I looked up at her through my eyelashes a thousand times.

I wondered if I should just ask her if she

hated me now. But I was sure she did and I didn't really want to know the answer because it was super-definitely yes.

Sarah looked at me with a weird innocent-but-evil look on her face. I can't figure out *what* she is thinking half the time.

Charlie and Daniel waved at me a few times from their desk, and I smiled back. And before the bell went for lunch, Charlie held up his whiteboard with Mr. Philpot's formula written on it to remind me.

HUNGER + NAUGHTY KID WHO'S NOT SORRY

= TOP BLOWN

GOOD LUCK!

Have you ever noticed that when you try to do something extra carefully, you end up doing the

complete opposite?

I was trying to knock extra carefully on Mr. Philpot's door, not too hard and not so lightly that he wouldn't hear me. Just the right amount of sound, like the perfectly angelic, good kid that I needed to show him I was. But I was trying so hard to get it right that I tripped over my own foot and ended up slamming my whole body against the door. I froze in horror, thinking the worst, but, thank goodness, Mr. Philpot opened the door with a mouth full of tuna pasta, and I said sorry right away.

Charlie's formula was correct, and I somehow spent the hour with Mr. Philpot and lived to tell the tale. I had done it. I got through the whole terrible day, even with a full hour with Mr. Philpot. But I couldn't bear the thought that after the weekend I still had ANOTHER week of paying for something I didn't do.

CHAPTER 19

That weekend, I tried to do the things I normally do and enjoy them as much as I normally do, but I just couldn't.

I imagined what the newspapers would be writing about me if I was famous enough. I was certain I now knew how famous people felt when papers printed lies.

I made a fake newspaper story to pass the time, drawing myself as a supervillain, with the headline:

Did you notice? Maro, my villain name, is Omar with the "O" at the end instead of the beginning.

All of it made me feel a bit villainy inside for real. So I set Esa up for my plan to catch him by saying I was going to the yard to play but quietly sneaking back into my room and under my bed.

Sure enough, after a bit, Esa whizzed in.

I waited a few seconds for him to grab the astronaut cards in his little fingers before I pounced on him.

"Ha! Got you! Why have you been doing this, Esa?" I said, putting my arms around him so he couldn't run away.

"Esa's funny," he said, grinning. "Esa's very, very funny."

I LAUGHED.
"Yes, Esa is funny."

At that moment, Maryam poked her head around the door and said, "Bwahahaha, he's my minion! The smartest pranksters always have help!"

"Hahaha, I knew it! You got me. I really believed you when Mrs. Rogers said she was your alibi!" I said.

"That's because I wasn't lying. It wasn't actually me. I made Esa do it."

"The pond thing wasn't actually me, but nobody believes me," I said, hanging my head.

"That's because you're not as cute as me," Maryam said, putting on her strawberry lip gloss. "Nice?" she asked, rubbing her lips together.

"Yes," I said. And funnily enough, she believed me.

•   •   •

Sunday was worse, because it was only one more sleep till school, and SCIENCE SUNDAY reminded me of the goo powder we had used last week.

I wondered what Allah was doing with His plan. He definitely always helps me when I'm in a mess, but I couldn't figure out how He would help me this time. There was just no way of proving I didn't wreck the pond.

I kept whispering to Him:

I know you're there.
I know you're going to help me.
Dad said you don't ever need
to take days off like we do.

Mrs. Rogers came over to cheer me up, and we played cards with Mom and Dad and planned to watch the news report on *mindfulness* that was filmed at our school.

My family packed themselves onto one sofa, super excited that they were going to see my little interview on TV.

When it started, we talked most of the way through, recognizing different spots in the school and saying things like:

"Look! There's Mrs. Hutchinson."

"Oh my gosh, there's Charlie in the background. Why is he walking like a robot?"

We watched as Sarah proudly said her bit about how mindfulness had changed her life. And how Jayden said everyone should learn mindfulness like they learn to walk.

And when I came on, everyone said,

"Shhhhhhh. Shh. OK, SHHHH!"

and flapped their hands around to make sure everyone was quiet.

It turns out I did speak in English!

"I'm so proud of you, Omar," said Mom.

And Dad messed up my hair to say the same without any words.

Mr. McLeary was being interviewed next, and the camera moved to a new spot in the playground.

"Oh . . . there's the pond in the background," I noticed sadly.

But, as he spoke and we watched, we all saw something that made our jaws drop and changed the world as we knew it.

Clear as day, there was Adam, with five bags of goo powder, pouring them quickly into the pond, looking around and running off!

CHAPTER 20

"HOORAY! THERE'S YOUR PROOF! This CHANGES EVERYTHING! Thank You, Allah!" said Dad,

throwing me over his shoulders and parading

me around the room.

"Everyone in the school must have just

watched that happen!" said Mom.

"Those stinky puddles of vomit will be sorry

now," said Maryam.

"I want ice cream!" said Esa.

"I want sweet potatoes," said Mrs. Rogers.

I didn't know what to say. It was crazy! I had been in so much trouble for what felt like months even though it had only been days, and the proof had just fallen out of the sky when I was least expecting it.

"Thank you, Allah," I whispered.

Dad kept running around the house with me over his shoulders, and I really, really laughed like I hadn't done for days.

Of course, the phone started ringing nonstop, as Charlie and Daniel, who had also seen what had happened on TV, wanted to talk about it.

. . .

On Monday morning, I felt really shy walking into the school, although I couldn't wait to sit next to my friends and have a normal lunchtime in the playground.

Poor Adam. I wondered what would happen to him. He'd probably take my place in Mr. McLeary's office at lunchtime.

I walked up to Mrs. Hutchinson awkwardly in the line as we waited to go into school and said, "Do you still hate me now?"

"Oh, Omar. Sweet child. No. No, no, I never hated you. How could I?" she said, her hair looking shocked at the question. "To tell you the truth . . . I mean, I'm not supposed to tell you the truth . . . but since you're thinking something so upsetting, I must say something . . . I never believed you did it.

And I tried to tell Mr. McLeary, but he didn't want to listen. I just had a *gut* *Feeling* it wasn't you, and I couldn't even look at you because of how sad you were and how much I couldn't help."

"Oh . . ." I managed. My heart swelled like a balloon in my chest.

I wanted to hug her, but you're not really allowed to hug teachers, and all my classmates would think I was a big baby, so I just stood there while the balloon tried to force its way up my throat and into a hot, relieved tear on my cheek.

Charlie and Daniel might as well have been holding signs that said:

183

Because they had the most excited energy
I've ever seen them with. Daniel took my hand
and waved it in the air for me like I had just
won a boxing match.

"Mr. McLeary wants to see you in his office first thing, Omar," said Mrs. Hutchinson, smiling.

"Where's Adam?" said Daniel as we walked into the school building. "He let you take the blame the whole time. I'll turn him into mashed broccoli."

Adam was in the principal's office. Well, he was outside it, waiting to come in after Mr. McLeary talked to me.

Mr. McLeary had a strange look on his face, the way he might look if his pants had fallen down while he was talking to the whole entire school.

"Omar, I've been thinking about what to say to you, but honestly I have no words. I'm so, so sorry for accusing you of something you didn't do. I'm very impressed at how much you care about your friends, and at how maturely you have taken this unfair punishment."

"It's OK, sir," I said.

"No, no, it's not OK. I basically called you a fungus-filled tomato."

I giggled. "You kind of did . . ."

"Well, I'd like to call you something else instead," he said, and pulled out a framed certificate from his drawer with my photo on it, which said:

BRILLIANT STUDENT AWARD.

But he didn't hand it to me. He said, "I've called your parents in for an assembly today and I'd like to give it to you then, in front of the whole school."

I beamed. I forgave him right there. He *was* really sorry.

Next, he called Adam in to apologize to me.

"Why did you do it?" I asked.

"Well . . . it was so cool that you were a hero. Nobody ever ignored you, and everyone wanted to give you stuff and hang out with you. So I kind of thought that maybe if I got you into trouble and then took the blame, then I could be a hero, too. AN EVEN BIGGER HERO.

At this point he grinned awkwardly and carried on. "But then I lost my nerve. It was too scary. I didn't want to be in trouble the way you were. I'm not brave enough to have lunch in here . . ." he said, looking at Mr. McLeary out of the corners of his petrified eyes.

I felt kind of sorry for him, so as we walked back to the classroom, I smiled and said, "You know, he's less scary if you imagine maggots falling out of his mouth whenever he talks."

The assembly was  times a gazillion!

Mr. McLeary and Mrs. Hutchinson made a big show of giving me the Brilliant Student Award, which wasn't even a thing in our school until now.

They projected a very cheesy picture of me from when I was judging the talent contest onto the wall and played the theme song from a film called *Top Gun* from the olden days, which made Mom and Dad and Mrs. Rogers go absolutely nuts and made me look like some kind of jet-plane-flying, world-saving hero.

YUCK! HAHAHAHA!

I looked around at everyone I loved, my family, my friends, my teachers. Even Mr. Philpot was enjoying himself.

Who am I kidding? It was the most

embarrassing, super-best assembly of my life!

ZANIB MIAN grew up in London and still lives there today. She was a science teacher for a few years after leaving university, but right from when she was a little girl, her passion was writing stories and poetry. She has released lots of picture books with the independent publisher Sweet Apple Publishers, but the Planet Omar series is the first time she's written for older readers.

KYAN CHENG is currently residing in Bristol with her husband and furbaby pup. One of her favorite things to do growing up was drawing characters from books and TV shows. She now has fun creating her own characters and continues to explore her favorite themes, which include nature, food and all creatures great and small.

THE NEXT

ADVENTURE IS
COMING SOON!

PLANET OMAR BOOKS ARE OUT OF THIS WORLD!